W9-CMD-661

Early and Middle Childhood
Education Department
The Ohio State University at Newark

For Richard

ONE GORILLA

A Counting Book

Atsuko Morozumi

Farrar, Straus & Giroux
New York

Here is a list of things I love.
One gorilla.

Two butterflies among the flowers and one gorilla.

Three budgerigars in my house
and one gorilla.

Four squirrels in the woods
and one gorilla.

Five pandas in the snow
and one gorilla.

Six rabbits in a field
and one gorilla.

Seven frogs by the fence
and one gorilla.

Eight fish in the sea
and one gorilla.

Nine birds among the leaves
and one gorilla.

Ten cats in my garden
and one gorilla.

10 cats

9 birds

8 fish

7 frogs

6 rabbits

5 pandas

4 squirrels

3 budgerigars

2 butterflies

But where is my gorilla?

Ah, there he is.